Black Moon by ~~~~~~ **reviews**

You've heard these sharp, dark and evocative words of Eugen Bacon's flash fiction—in your dreams or darker visions—but don't know it until you read them, and find they gnaw at your subconscious, demanding to be recalled.
– Craig Cormick, award-winning author of *Years of the Wolf*

~~~

Dark, beautiful, chilling and surreal glimpses of life, love, death and beyond. Poetic and exquisite, these heart-searing fantastical tales will linger and haunt you long after you have put them down.
– Steven Paulsen, award-winning author of *Shadows on the Wall*

~~~

Black Moon is not what you expect. The short fictions are bright as eyes glimpsed in an abandoned house, sharp as wounds, quivering with uncanny metamorphoses. Words and images conspire to imply narrative pathways, before tripping your helpless imagination into its darkest recesses. You turn around and there's nothing there, but it is the nothing that has always followed you, invisible. *Black Moon* is not what you expect, but you feel its breath, clammy on your neck, and it's much too late to go back now.
– Oz Hardwick, award-winning poet and academic

~~~

A treasure chest of dark imaginings destined to beguile, with words and illustrations that will hold you prisoner. Prepare to meet the sharp embrace of enchanted dreams, each a perfect alchemy of the uncanny and the real.
Every piece of flash fiction in *Black Moon* displays a clarity of vision that skewers the everyday with the fearless thrust of 'what if'.
– Clare E Rhoden, author of the *Chronicles of the Pale* series

Here's a collection of strange fragments that illuminate how realities shift from moment to moment, how different points of perspective transform the experience of the world. Anything goes: child as victim or adventurer; houses and men that shapeshift; the creepy dolls that are making their own plans. These flash fictions, and the evocative images that accompany them, shimmer with the awareness that we can never fully understand the world, never pin it down. Let yourself enter its space; know you will emerge changed.
– Jen Webb, distinguished author, poet and academic

~~~

Black Moon is a beguiling, evocatively illustrated combination of flash fiction, speculative fiction and prose poetry, shaped by a weird, sometimes dark imagination and a pithy, explorative eloquence.
– Paul Hetherington, award-winning Australian poet and academic

~~~

This slim volume of dark speculative flash fiction shimmers with unsettling and memorable images. Eugen Bacon's words subtly subvert our expectations on every page, as Elena Betti's illustrations blur rather than draw the line between fantasy and reality. *Black Moon* is a vivid, mysterious and magical space rooted in the detail of everyday life. It will resonate with the reader long after the book is set aside. Original and intense.
– Dominique Hecq, award-winning poet, novelist, short story writer and scholar.

An IFWG Publishing Chapbook

Black Moon

Graphic Speculative Flash Fiction

by Eugen Bacon

Illustrated by Elena Betti

This is a work of fiction. The events and characters portrayed herein are imaginary and are not intended to refer to specific places, events or living persons. The opinions expressed in this manuscript are solely the opinions of the author and do not necessarily represent the opinions of the publisher.

Printed in Palatino Linotype and FreightNeo Pro.

IFWG Publishing International

www.ifwgpublishing.com

Acknowledgements

To the Prose Poetry Project, International Poetry Studies Institute, University of Canberra—thank you for offering a safe but addictive space to explore microlit as a hybrid of poetry and flash fiction.

To artist and illustrator Elena Betti for accurately rendering my vision.

To publisher Gerry Huntman of IFWG for believing in that vision, and making it happen.

For the stories we yearn to tell, the diversity of our voices. I am many, betwixt, a sum of cultures.

Monument

Eons of merry jingles in a disrepaired world closed with the release of a redacted report.

The numbed lyric took to chanting slogans.

Now she stands sentry, a silent tombstone.

Musk In Their Scent

Silent, in plain sight.

It was not a chronicle of love, but of war. They understood humankind's fault, its love for shiny objects.

Iridescent eyes that shifted like opals serenaded men and women before dusk fell and ghouls snatched souls.

Fingerprint Of A Curse

The nacreous moon toppled from the sky in spectral cartwheel and splashed into a black river as the town slept.

Trapped in the time capsule of a hound's howl.

What The Window Saw

The curious window unhinged from the pane of a house that bordered a thicket in the east and a hillock that fell to a gruff coast in the west.

She shadowed a toddler clasping a candy man's hand, walking away into the woods.

Torn jeans and a t-shirt, his jacket the colour of dirty trees. Her charcoal curls, his grey mop, the girl cast a backward glance, her tiny palm wrapped in his fist until the maw of the thicket swallowed them.

When the candy man shapeshifted to become the bogey man, the bewildered window floundered back to her house and locked herself to an infinity of crystal tears.

The Real Deal

We're making winged centurions to signal Enough.

We hate babies rolled out on gurneys inside body bags.
We say No to little girls with bones that snap through
hungry skin. Detached women who stampede over
them in a dash to the snarl of a bog river that no more
runs. Silent men with eyes blank as buttons in a world
muted by homophobes, supremacists, anti-Semites,
fat-pocketed politicians and sleek-eyed priests.

And Yes to the infinity of iron-clad vigilantes with wings
meting out justice to unspecified ills. Soon we must
staple them to our souls and brandish daggers against
those who throw bones.

We're making /centurions: that are/ neither persons
nor poems [but rather dirges: elegy. hymn. chant] to
signal *trop c'est trop*. Solemn, this procession.

We Admire Your Hopefulness

We salute you, tunic-clad woman in sandals reclined on a bed, your Venus hair finely roped.

A plunging neckline caresses your breasts all the way to meet a waist sash.

Oh, the measure of your grace.

Behind the glamour of chandelier earrings and golden anklets, what song of silence will climb out of those eyes /blistered with verse/ swelled with eons [/ˈiːən/ *noun* 1. epoch 2. philosophy] of lamentation?

Regret, but always forgiveness, for irredeemable savages the world has spawned. Fragmented bodies, crimsoned walls.

Timing Is Everything
In A Social Order

The first thing we felt were clouds like conjoined pillows swollen with grey foam. We needed to experience summer, in particular an Irishman. We found him in Dublin, a curly-haired certainty who rolled his RRRs. He was tall and lanky, guzzled waRm beer like a hose. He was a host on some headline, was available that night with a different level of passion that was a peRsonal inteRRRaction, to the detriment of us. So I got up and gobbled the cat, but our sudden distance still made no sense.

Damaged Beyond Words

Phone zombies, incapable of loving, meander across the
streets in a smear of shapes, a rain of fate. Disenchanted
with life, they shadow frenetic social media in tweets
that never look like missing. As lightning strikes, winter
falls, the silent march is a drum circle. Dogs yap yap as
the zombies stalk our planet, eyes glued on their smart
phones, uncaring to gravity, friction or genuity as real
people pass them by.

A Profound Wonder

He stepped back into his body and wondered who would find him, when?

The world was too busy obsessed with the trending #Thanos #Salah #Thrones, he'd be porridge before anyone thought to miss him.

He would first turn into a blot and then a gruel, sickly green and oozy, a melt of bile…

As a random stranger someplace else picked herself up and was astonished to find a new friend request tucked inside notifications. Celebrated the new connection with a few hearts and hashtags, tweeting until dawn. #WhiteHouse #Bachelorette #MeToo

She Was Together

…with her companions when she found him in a sea of bones, a big-eyed child with a thatch of hair.

She lit a pyre and belly-danced through dusk, as he pranced along.

Revelling birth. Or death.

She curled herself around the boy before dawn, to protect him from early transfiguration.

When wind was no more a whisper, she wept on his chest and he breathed fire to put out her tears.

Leap!

How high he soared.

More Than He Bargained For

As he wrote the world in its solemn clarity, each stroke of his pen brought a thing to life.

Like the mage who loved vignettes, their spontaneity and sudden finding, their fascination with relatability. It was a coming to know, where the long or short of each literary fragment was a cornerstone of being. So he tucked story cocktails in three pearls for the newborn. A black one, to dispel demons that snatched away sleep. A pink one, to discern evil when dancing with a stranger. A mauve one, to spot fiendry or divinity embedded in politics. It was the chuckle from the child's belly, her coo and kroo to locate the milk and honey in these gifts, that gave a taste of promise to the tucked away stories. And the /mage who had waited/ a lifetime: for a brand new activist [*noun*: 1. apostle. 2. fanatic. 3. visionary] understood that a confounding chronicle was writing itself.

Or like the man who took bits of a girl little by little.

Until one day she looked at the mirror, and all she saw was a gnarled tree with frayed leaves on its crown.

Or like the man who was a timeless sleeper in other realms, but an urn harnessed him into the attic of a

cottage in a small farming village. And though he was ash, he was once a skull pregnant with mould. He reminisced about language, its place in bones suspended in rope away from a briny abyss.

Somewhere down the cottage, culinary sounds of plague, shame and desire banned from other worlds in contentious steps to make or erase history long after sea change, in the betterment of the universe.

Moments Become Games

The man at a forsaken beach was solemn then he smiled.

The gloss in his teeth struck a passer-by like lightning, rendered her helpless.

His breath of corpses, but fangs like stars as he gored her skin.

An Unnamed Story

At first, she attributed the cramps to the tightness of her corset.

Then she realised it was her period.

But what collapsed onto her sanitary pad was a little creature, then another, little flies with eyes and human ears, bleeding and bleeding out of her until the horror of blood begot a beast.

A Winter Masterpiece

The dirge was one of a kind. It waltzed over a fence, pirouetted to the black wail. Starlight on her face. Ice in her core. Forever and a day, an enveloping pain swollen with sweet melodies.

She couldn't decide what to do with her heart: so she laid it on a garland of new flowers on a grave. Took no notice of the walking dead that sought memory or touch, tore herself from the wish she left behind.

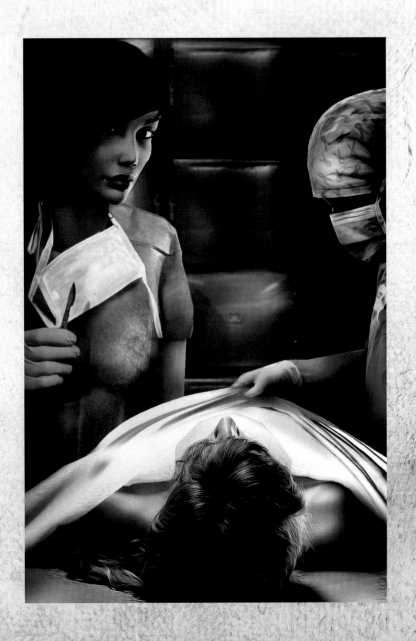

She Asked the Mortician

…to wrench Shane's gold teeth and a blacksmith to solder them into an amulet. Together with her wedding ring.

A stand of Joshua trees enshrouded her in the desert, her chant rising to a crescendo as she beseeched the rare blood moon. Aargh, whaa! The rough bark of crows.

Saltwater and copper, her blood to his and her artefacts.

When he emerged, he showed his true self. The rot in his words begot goblins with rancid manuscripts that meowled like kittens and chased into the night.

Dark, quiet, the trees watched as he fed on her platelets.

He Could Talk Under Water

The subject refused to stay silent, so we experimented with immersion. First, he grew gills and swam about the coffin-shaped tank like a fish.

But years of wanting freedom can take a toll. As depression set in, he stopped eating the bread crumbs we put in and his gills began to seal.

One day there was a wet sound, a rattle or a gurgle, and he was thrusting in the water with a surge of strength. He shook violently a whole minute. Then he stopped moving.

He floated face down moments before he sank. It took two weeks for a release of gas that ballooned him to the surface, fingers fat as bratwursts, but pale like poached whiting.

The smell of death... the taste, touch and sight of it. Do you know hearing is the last sense you lose?

Cinders in Her Hair

Between summer and autumn, she satisfied a temporary wanting by turning a whole school into cinders.

Was it the malevolence of bitch girls and the opulence ranking of their homes? The spite of segregating boys and the falsity of their supremacy?

Books shrieked and collapsed from library shelves, and the science lab drew a last breath before it swooned.

Was it the unsolvable maze of the geography lesson and its roots and shoots, creative sustainability: tuning to animals, people and the environment?

A school is just a school—when its teachers and students burn, it is nothing. She washed petrol off her hands as the blaze crisped bodies like overcooked turkeys unscripted in a barbeque.

Was it to satisfy a curiosity about how human bodies blister and scorch? The scientist at heart tossed a match and held dominion over life and death, as orange flames roared in her eyes.

It's Safer in Her Head

…than it is in nameless streets where rivers bleed—
they don't stand quiet in pyjama tops. She knows the
world when it all goes shit, haemorrhaging waters
hungry for language. She speaks to a moment but no
love unfolds—just bullets tearing hearts in a cosmos
history will judge.

It's safer in her head.

If Looks Could Kill

Case Study: M

It's all about growing the resilient child, safeguarding them against depression. The Self Esteem Movement has all the slogans for psychologically immunised behaviour.

M's mother did everything right that was nothing to do with the secret life of a zoo.

So who was that creature and her piercing gaze, no reflexive emotion, even if someone were to gift her with a gilded box of truffles from the Land of Two Suns?

She sat in the basement, feet facing her mother who to all appearances was asleep, save for a smashed head, splodged with an egg yolk of brain matter—not the grey-white kind you might find pickled in a lab or at the back of a butcher's store—and the delicate pink of leaked blood, plastered with skull.

There was no evidence of an instrument that could cause such degree of blunt force trauma.

And some members of the forensic crew contaminated

the scene, falling to their knees and clutching their heads, moaning of a terrible and bizarre migraine that strangely dissipated upon exiting the basement.

Like a Dog with a Bone

A spectre imprints on its subject, and you don't just shake it.

It follows you everywhere, invisible, and you don't notice it by the curtains as you shower, out the door and into the bus on the way to your next appointment, all day in your everyday. You can't just shake it.

Sometimes you will notice the hum of the aircon long after you turn it off. The iron box plugged back on, but you didn't do it. The cistern running water, and then it flushes itself. A light bulb that keeps cracking, no matter how many times you replace it. A coldness in the room even in the heart of summer. A shadow at the edge of your 20:20 vision. A wisp on your nape, you turn and there's nothing there.

Sometimes sprinkling holy water or avoiding lizards that cross your path might do it. You could try burning sage around the perimeter of the house. But to rid yourself of one, to really rid yourself of a spectre, you must understand its creation and appease or eliminate its cause.

You might need the help of a psychic.

But whatever you do: remember, always remember, that once a spectre imprints on you, it's like a dog. It will snarl, gnarl, bite harder at the bone.

The Replacements

Pea's cat Luna nearly had kittens, but two pushed out stillborn and the third came out squirming, all covered in bloodied slime. It mewled, deaf, blind and scrabbling, wonky and too feeble to reach a tit.

Its fumbles and woeful wail so irked the cat, she finally ate it. As if carnivorous wasn't enough, Luna left half on the fleece snuggle bed, a midriff tear—ginger and white its head and paws—lips curled in a final rage at a delinquent mother.

Pea found the toys at an antique place. There was a shop front and in she went. It was sandwiched between a café and a butcher shop. The touristy-crafty shop was swollen with bric-a-brac: Christmas ornaments, canning jars, tarnished silverware, 70s guitars, crocheted gowns, a cursed record player, a knitting gnome… and twin dolls.

Pea thought the dolls might cheer the cat, replace the two kittens that had died, not the one she had eaten. Bad. Luna. No!

But there was something about the twins. One wore graphite hair and a yellow sundress. The other was an afro-haired boy.

Pea liked them for herself.

She sat them in the master bedroom and could have sworn they silently watched at a vantage point atop the chiffonier, one upon which Luna once loved to perch and purr and curl herself to sleep.

Downstairs in the kitchen Luna was doing a back-hunched, leg-rub thing. Purrr. Purrr. Weaving through, head-butting and nuzzling Pea's leg. "Go on make some friends," she shooed the cat.

Somewhere between the nut and berry tones of an organic espresso, and the stacking of a dishwasher, Pea heard a terrible yowl like someone was killing the cat. She leapt up the stairs, but there was nothing stalking or harming the cat. There was no cat. Just the silent gaze of twin dolls in her room.

Something about the dolls—always watching. As Pea and Frank undressed, took to bed and each burrowed into a book. Pea favoured Zola and Flaubert, Frank was Kafka and Hemingway.

Frank was boring as a bulletin, an executive who made policies that triggered or hindered progress to climate change, like that idea of genetic engineered lamb chops. But someone shot it down.

Nightly without fail, at 9.31pm precisely, Frank carefully placed a bookmark and snapped the book shut. Took his glasses off and laid them on the side table. Rested the book by the side table, leaned on his elbow, faced Pea and said, "Okay."

This act peeved her—what was okay? He said it like it was a response to a question or a statement.

Okay. The hell?!

Despite her rile, she would take off her underclothing, rub lubricant on his already erect body—after reading Kafka?—and stay quiet as he hauled her to his need.

He grunted like a hog. Sometimes she used a dildo and these times she came for real.

The dolls watched all this and more. Listened, like when Frank attempted dialogue. When he thumbed a page of *The Metamorphosis*, lifted his spectacles and said, "Babe, what happened to the cat?"

Pea could have sworn the girl doll cocked her head. Did the boy smile?

Sure thing, what happened to Luna? Last Pea saw the cat was the day she shooed her from leg nuzzles, same day the dolls came home from the touristy-crafty shop. Same dolls that watched.

And watched…

Patiently waiting…

Waiting…

To replace her and Frank.

The Book of Unfinished Parables

If you were one of us, would you be the agent on the other end of the insurance line, paying attention with a smile for clues that ranked each claim?

Would you be the checkout guy at the supermarket, the one who scanned and packed, scanned and packed, processed payment, scanned and packed… start to end of shift… watching the world come and go?

Would you be the kindergarten sub, fresh from a diploma and a working with children check, the gluten intolerant one always relied on to arrive on time?

What if you were a child? The plump-legged baby wearing spectacles in a pram… Or the wrecking boy with a bloody nose and a toad in his schoolbag… Or the pig-tailed girl with a pinafore and a splintered wrist from the monkey bars…

Or perhaps you're the puppet mistress, a voodoo queen with dolls, water and high voltage, the conductor of epidemics, quakes and cyclones—manifestations of battle that rose from the Garden of Eden.

Temperatures Soared In The City

…and melted pear tree blossoms coated with frost.

The book, seduced by climate change, found its way into a tavern that had a dragon and a fresh-faced human, despite his stubble, and he was kissing a pint of ale.

The book struck up a buddyhood with the man whose name was Weed, Shriek or Creek, and he was waiting for a shade.

The shade arrived and she was pretty as tourmaline, dressed in a bloodshot bare-all. But she had the voice of a bad violin—tone dead and unbright. At intervals it woke up and went shrill.

They talked all night about the literature of villains, but the heat couldn't be beat, and it brewed their minds for all that happened when the clock struck twelve.

Unlearning the Sea

The landlocked mermaid submerges her singing voice in a freshwater jar capped with memories of the humping sea and its giddy waves.

Drowning melodies bubble to the surface, but suffocate.

If it rains, she gets wet. She understands the value of water, spears into navy blue ripples of chlorinated pools. Hydrogen and oxygen molecules infused with hydrogen chloride and sodium chlorine—salt nowhere near the levels in the sea.

Every night inside her bathtub, she dreams of pearls that embalm her into a forever sleep.

Her Name Is Soho

Feline eyes, body ripped like a panther.

Jungle scent, like wet animal fur. All accentuate her wilderness as she lies with him.

But he can never reach her.

She is not of this world. No soother of hearts, dead inside as a gravestone.

It's All In The Plan

The emerald-eyed witch wore the face of a girl, but was an impossible love.

So he sacrificed his dove-eyed wife, buried her secret in the soul of botany.

And plucked fresh blooms for his fiery enchantress.

Hugging a Tree Until
She Doesn't

She rearranges her beauty, first her hair and then her shape, to erase a memory.

The surgeon's scalpel cuts a bit here and a bit there, killing the plundered teen inside.

But she remembers limericks of sun and light, even as she slaughters first her lovers, then their wives.

By the time she reaches the children, her blade has dissolved into a poetic horizon.

Eugen Bacon is African Australian, a computer scientist mentally re-engineered into creative writing. She's the author of *Claiming T-Mo* by Meerkat Press and *Writing Speculative Fiction* by Red Globe Press, Macmillan.

Eugen's work has won, been shortlisted, longlisted or commended in national and international awards, including the Bridport Prize, Copyright Agency Prize, Australian Shadows Awards, Ditmar Awards and Nommo Award for Speculative Fiction by Africans.

Website: www.eugenbacon.com

Twitter: @EugenBacon